MW01094357

Disney · PIXAR

ELEMENTAL

THE GRAPHIC NOVEL

Random House 🏠 New York

rhcbooks.com

ISBN 978-0-7364-4376-0 (trade) — ISBN 978-0-7364-4377-7 (ebook)

Printed in the United States of America

10 9 8 7 6 5 4 3 2 1

DISNEY · PIXAR

ELEMENTAL

THE GRAPHIC NOVEL

Random House 🏠 New York

EMBER
Lumen

The smart and hotheaded daughter of immigrants, **EMBER LUMEN** has grown up in her father's store in Firetown. She knows that one day, she will take over the family business and fulfill her father's dream. But after a chance encounter with an easygoing Water Element named Wade Ripple, Ember feels a new spark inside her begin to burn brightly. Will she be forced to choose between being the perfect daughter and following her own dreams?

Meet the CHARACTERS

BERNIE
Lumen

When he was a young Fire Element, **BERNIE** left Fire Land with his wife, Cinder, for a bright future in Element City. There he found that Fire Elements don't mix well with Air, Water, and Earth Elements. Settling in Firetown, Bernie and Cinder welcomed their only child, Ember, as Bernie worked hard to create a business honoring the traditions of Fire Land. He hopes to one day hand the shop over to Ember.

Meet the CHARACTERS

▲▲ CINDER
Lumen

When she arrived in Firetown with her husband, Bernie, strong-willed **CINDER** established her own business—a matchmaking service.
She has a natural gift for knowing if a Fire Element is in love, just by smelling their smoke!
While she plays matchmaker to the community, her biggest concern is her daughter, Ember, who just can't make a match—no matter how determined Cinder might be to find her a flame.

Meet the CHARACTERS

WADE
Ripple

WADE RIPPLE, an emotional Water Element, spends his days as a city inspector, tracking down a series of mysterious water leaks in Element City. And he's perfect for the job! But during his investigation, he meets the fiery Ember Lumen. He wonders if it's possible for a Water Element and a Fire Element—two opposites that definitely don't mix—to forge a friendship.

Meet the CHARACTERS

BROOK
Ripple

Wade's loving mom, **BROOK RIPPLE**, supports her family with care and compassion. Just like her son (and, well, everyone else in her family), Brook loves a good cry. In fact, for game nights, the whole family plays the Crying Game, trying to make each other cry. As a successful architect, Brook knows talent when she sees it, and spies something special in Ember.

Meet the CHARACTERS

GALE
Cumulus

An avid fan of Element City's Windbreakers airball team, **GALE CUMULUS** is Wade's boss at City Hall. It might seem like this Air Element has strong opinions and is full of, well, hot air, but don't be fooled. Gale has a good heart and wants to do the right thing. When Wade and Ember go to Gale for help, her strong sense of fairness and willingness to find the best solution for everyone make all the difference.

Meet the **CHARACTERS**

FERN GROUCHWOOD

FERN
Grouchwood

As his name suggests, **FERN GROUCHWOOD** isn't the friendliest Earth Element. Sarcastic, dry, and covered in vines and leaves, Fern works in the processing department at City Hall on permits that can make or break a business. When Ember's father's shop is put in danger by a leaky pipe incident, Fern is not very helpful.

A NEW DAY DAWNS ON ELEMENT CITY...

...AS A SHIP ARRIVES, BRINGING HOPEFUL PEOPLE FROM ACROSS THE WORLD TO ITS SHORES...

PEOPLE LIKE CINDER...

...AND BERNIE, FROM FIRE LAND.

OUR NEW HOME, MY CHILD."

"TRANSLATED FROM THE FIRISH LANGUAGE.

ATTENTION, PASSENGERS! WE ARE APPROACHING THE PORT OF ENTRY. PLEASE PREPARE TO DISEMBARK.

AS BERNIE AND CINDER DEPART, THEY SEE PEOPLE OF ALL KINDS, LIKE EARTH PEOPLE...

...WATER PEOPLE...

OOPS! I BELIEVE THIS IS YOURS.

THANKS! HAVE A WETTER DAY!

...AND AIR PEOPLE.

WELCOME, BERNIE AND CINDER, TO ELEMENT CITY!

WELCOME, MY EMBER, TO YOUR NEW LIFE.

TIME PASSES. AS EMBER GROWS, SHE LEARNS HER FAMILY'S CUSTOMS...

OUR BLUE FLAME HOLDS ALL OF OUR TRADITIONS AND GIVES US STRENGTH TO BURN BRIGHT.

...AND BERNIE BUILDS THE STORE OF HIS DREAMS.

THIS SHOP IS THE *DREAM* OF OUR FAMILY. AND SOMEDAY IT WILL ALL BE YOURS.

FIREPLACE

FINALLY, BERNIE'S SHOP OPENS, AND THE FIRST CUSTOMER ENTERS.

WELCOME! EVERYTHING HERE IS AUTHENTIC.

THEN I GOTTA TRY THE KOL NUTS!

KOL NUT, COMING UP!

HA!

GOOD DAUGHTER.

SOMEDAY THIS SHOP WILL ALL BE MINE!

WHEN YOU ARE READY.

STILL MORE TIME PASSES, AND MORE FIRE PEOPLE ARRIVE! BUT THERE ARE PROBLEMS...

SEE? DANGER!

THE CANALS FULL OF WATER IN THIS PART OF TOWN POSE A THREAT TO THE FIRE ELEMENTS. SO...

OKAY, SHUT IT DOWN!

...THE WATER FLOWING TO FIRETOWN IS CUT OFF. A LEAK IN BERNIE'S SHOP FINALLY STOPS!

OKAY!

AS EMBER GROWS UP, SHE LEARNS FOR HERSELF THAT WATER CAN POSE OTHER PROBLEMS...

WATER. KEEP AN EYE ON THEM.

AH!

YOU SPLASH IT, YOU BUY IT!

MORE TIME PASSES, UNTIL ONE DAY...

ÀSHFÁ,* CUSTOMER.

*FIRISH FOR "FATHER"

HOW ABOUT... *YOU* TAKE IT TODAY.

FOR REAL?

RÂÎ KHÎF!* HOW CAN I HELP YOU?

ALL THIS, AND SPARKLERS ARE BUY ONE, GET ONE FREE?

*FIRISH FOR "WELCOME!"

THAT'S RIGHT!

GREAT! I'LL TAKE THE FREE ONE.

OH NO, SEE, YOU NEED TO *BUY* ONE TO GET ONE *FREE*.

BUT I JUST WANT THE *FREE* ONE.

HMM?

EMBER FOLLOWS WADE ONTO THE TRAIN HEADING TOWARD THE CITY...

...THE TRAIN THAT EMBER *SWORE* SHE'D NEVER TAKE. BUT NOW SHE HAS NO CHOICE.

THE TRAIN ARRIVES IN ELEMENT CITY...BUT AS EMBER DISCOVERS, IT ISN'T BUILT FOR FIRE PEOPLE.

OOH, SORRY!

IN PURSUIT OF WADE, EMBER FACES OBSTACLE AFTER OBSTACLE. IS SHE TOO LATE?

NO NO NO NO NO NO!

JUST AS WADE SENDS IN HIS TICKETS, HE NOTICES EMBER'S LIGHT...

WHOA.

PLEASE! NO! YOU DON'T UNDERSTAND!

THE SHOP IS MY DAD'S *DREAM*. IF I'M THE REASON IT GETS SHUT DOWN...HE WILL NEVER TRUST ME TO TAKE OVER.

WATER. ALWAYS TRYING TO WATER US DOWN!

HE WAS A WATER *PERSON*, DAD, NOT JUST WATER.

SAME THING. AND WHY IS THERE WATER IN THE PIPES? THE CITY SHUT IT DOWN YEARS AGO. THERE SHOULD BE *NO WATER!*

COUGH COUGH

WE WILL GET THROUGH THIS. JUST LIKE *BEFORE.*

BEFORE?

THERE IS A REASON WE LEFT FIRE LAND.

OH, EMBER, IT WAS SO BEAUTIFUL THERE.

"HERE IN FIRETOWN, WE ARE THE ONLY FAMILY WITH A BLUE FLAME. BUT BACK HOME, *EVERY* FAMILY HAD ONE.

"YOUR FATHER PUT EVERYTHING WE HAD INTO STARTING OUR LIFE TOGETHER... BUT THEN A GREAT *STORM* CAME."

BERNIE MANAGED TO SAVE THE FAMILY'S BLUE FLAME...BUT EVERYTHING THEY HAD WORKED FOR WAS DESTROYED.

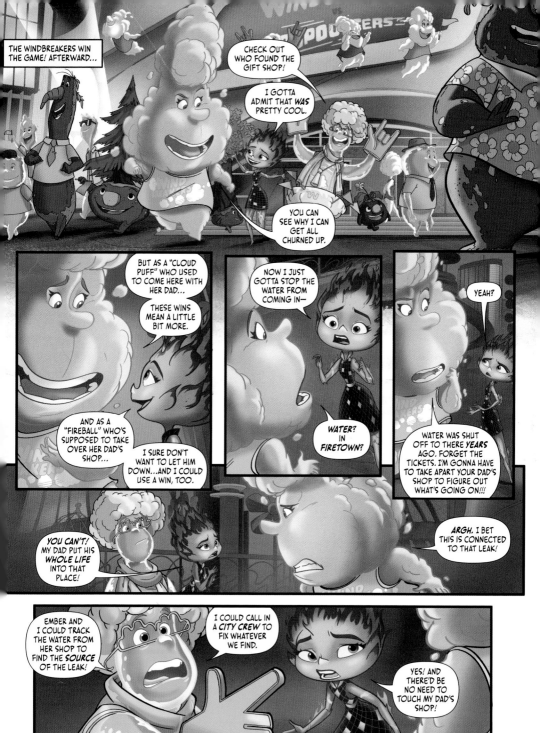

YOU'RE LUCKY YOU'RE A CUTE COUPLE.

OH, WE'RE NOT A—

YOU'VE GOT UNTIL FRIDAY TO FIND THE LEAK AND GET A CREW TO FIX IT. THEN THE TICKETS ARE FORGIVEN. IF NOT? YOUR DAD'S SHOP GETS *SHUT DOWN*.

EMBER AND WADE BEGIN THEIR SEARCH AT THE SHOP...

HOW COULD THE LEAK NOW BE WORSE?

NOW THAT WATER IS BACK, THE PRESSURE IS FORCING IT UP TO *ALL* YOUR PIPES.

HOW DID YOU EVEN END UP HERE?

"I WAS IN THE CANALS, CHECKING THE DOORS FOR LEAKS, WHEN I FOUND SOME WATER THAT SHOULDN'T HAVE BEEN THERE. IT WAS RUSTY, WITH A HINT OF...MOTOR OIL?

"THEN THERE WAS THIS *WHOOSH* OF WATER, AND I GOT SUCKED INTO A FILTERING SYSTEM...

"THEN I HEARD THIS EXPLOSION! THAT'S HOW I ENDED UP AT YOUR PLACE."

MY TEMPER CAUSED THIS.

THEY SEE A MOVIE...

...HIT UP A PHOTO BOOTH...

...AND TAKE IN THE VIEW OF ELEMENT CITY FROM ABOVE.

THEY EVEN TAKE A WALK AROUND MINERAL LAKE, WHERE...

WHOA. HOW'D YOU DO THAT?

IT'S THE MINERALS.

BUT WHILE EMBER AND WADE GET TO KNOW EACH OTHER BETTER, THE SANDBAGS GIVE WAY!

SO THE NEXT DAY...

NO NO NO NO NO NO!

FIREPLACE

THE WATER IS *BACK!*

BUT EVEN AS EMBER FIXES A LEAKY PIPE...

EMBER LUMEN? DELIVERY FOR EMBER LUMEN.

FLOWERS FOR EMBER?

OH, EXCUSE ME. HEH-HEH, THESE ARE BEAUTIFUL.

I'M GOING TO PUT THESE AWAY.

IN THE BASEMENT...

WHAT ARE YOU *DOING* HERE?

I GOT BAD NEWS. THE SANDBAGS DIDN'T HOLD.

UH, OBVIOUSLY!

I ALSO GOT WORSE NEWS...I FORGOT A *TINY* DETAIL ABOUT THE LAST TIME I SAW THAT CITY CREW.

COUGH COUGH

DAD, THOSE ARE TOO HOT.

I'M OKAY. I LOVE HOT FOOD.

ACTUALLY... IT'S REALLY TASTY IF YOU WATER IT DOWN A LITTLE...

WATER US DOWN? WATER US DOWN?!

WE WILL *NEVER* BE WATERED DOWN BY YOU. GET OUT!

ALL RIGHT, SIR. YOU GOTTA GO!

MEET ME AT THE BEACH AND WE'LL MAKE MORE SANDBAGS.

WE HAVE TO FIGURE OUT HOW TO FIX THOSE DOORS.

LATER THAT EVENING, AT THE BEACH...

I DON'T THINK THIS IS GOING TO WORK.

WELL, IT WON'T UNLESS YOU HOLD THE BAG STRAIGHT.

MAYBE YOUR DAD WILL UNDERSTAND. WITH MY DAD, WE WERE LIKE OIL AND WATER. I NEVER GOT A CHANCE TO FIX THAT.

BUT YOU GUYS ARE DIFFERENT.

IT MIGHT BE TIME TO TELL HIM.

YEAH, RIGHT. AND TELL HIM WHAT? THAT I GOT US SHUT DOWN AND *DESTROYED* HIS DREAM?!

I THINK I'M FAILING. MY ÀSHFÁ SHOULD HAVE RETIRED *YEARS* AGO, BUT HE DOESN'T THINK I'M READY.

YOU HAVE NO IDEA HOW HARD THEY'VE WORKED, OR WHAT THEY'VE HAD TO ENDURE, THE FAMILY THEY LEFT BEHIND...

HOW DO YOU REPAY A SACRIFICE THAT BIG?

I'M A BAD DAUGHTER.

HEY, NO. YOU'RE DOING YOUR BEST.

I'M A MESS.

NAH, I THINK YOU'RE EVEN MORE BEAUTIFUL.

MAYBE YOU WERE RIGHT WHEN YOU SAID MY TEMPER IS ME TRYING TO TELL ME SOMETHING.

WHOA, LOOK WHAT YOUR FIRE DID TO THE SAND. IT'S *GLASS*.

EMBER EXPERIMENTS WITH HER FLAME, CREATING WHAT SHE IS FEELING...

IT LOOKS LIKE A VIVISTERIA FLOWER.

I KNOW HOW TO SEAL THOSE DOORS!

SOON, AT THE CULVERT...

...EMBER USES HER FLAME TO TURN THE SAND INTO A GLASS WALL.

ARE YOU CRYING?

YES! I'VE JUST NEVER BEEN PUNCHED IN THE FACE WITH BEAUTY BEFORE.

IT WORKED!

I'LL HAVE GALE COME BY RIGHT AFTER WORK.

OH...HERE. I SAVED THIS FOR YOU. IT'S SPECIAL.

BACK AT THE SHOP IN FIRETOWN...

EMBER, I SEE A CHANGE IN YOU. YOU'RE HAPPIER. CALMER WITH CUSTOMERS. ALWAYS PUTTING THE SHOP FIRST.

YOU'VE PROVEN I CAN TRUST YOU. ≳COUGH COUGH≲

I'M SO LUCKY I HAVE YOU.

EMBER VISITS WADE TO SEE IF THERE IS ANY NEWS FROM GALE. HE INVITES HER TO HAVE DINNER WITH HIS FAMILY WHILE THEY WAIT FOR GALE TO CALL.

BUT UNKNOWN TO EMBER, HER MOTHER HAS FOLLOWED HER!

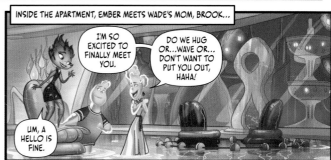

INSIDE THE APARTMENT, EMBER MEETS WADE'S MOM, BROOK...

I'M SO EXCITED TO FINALLY MEET YOU.

DO WE HUG OR...WAVE OR... DON'T WANT TO PUT YOU OUT, HAHA!

UM, A HELLO IS FINE.

...AND THE REST OF HIS FAMILY!

HEY, EVERYONE! THIS IS EMBER!

DURING DINNER, A GLASS PITCHER BREAKS. WITHOUT THINKING, EMBER SKILLFULLY REPAIRS IT INTO SOMETHING BEAUTIFUL... AND BROOK NOTICES HER TALENT.

AFTER DINNER, EMBER PLAYS THE CRYING GAME WITH WADE AND HIS FAMILY. BUT IN THIS GAME, YOU TRY *NOT* TO CRY!

YOU HAVE ONE MINUTE. GO!

1979. NOVEMBER. YOU WERE—

BWAHHHHHH!

OKAY, EMBER, WADE, YOU'RE UP!

YEAH, THIS IS ALMOST UNFAIR.

BECAUSE I HAVE LITERALLY NEVER CRIED.

YOU GOT NO CHANCE.

SOUNDS LIKE A CHALLENGE.

SUDDENLY...

DON'T MOVE!

MOM, IT'S OKAY. HE'S JUST A FRIEND.

SILENCE! FIRE AND WATER CANNOT BE TOGETHER!

I WILL PROVE IT! COME WITH ME.

SOON, AT CINDER'S MATCHMAKING OFFICE...

YOU MUST LIGHT THESE WITH YOUR FIRE, AND I WILL READ THE SMOKE.

FWOOSH

SEE, EMBER, IT CANNOT BE.

BUT WADE HAS A THOUGHT. USING EMBER'S LIGHT...

ACTUALLY...

CINDER? WHO'S DOWN THERE?

IT'S MY DAD! WADE, YOU HAVE TO GO!

WAIT, ARE WE A MATCH?

WHAT'S GOING ON? I WOKE UP AND NOBODY WAS UPSTAIRS.

IT WAS JUST ME. I WAS... DOUBLE-CHECKING THE LOCKS, AND MOM CAME DOWN, AND...

YES, AND WE...BEGAN LOOKING AT THIS DOOR.

WELL, I'M TOO EXCITED TO SLEEP. IN TWO DAYS... I'M RETIRING!

TWO DAYS?

OH, BERNIE!

WE'RE GOING TO THROW A *BIG* PARTY. A GRAND REOPENING.

THAT WAY I CAN TELL THE WHOLE WORLD THAT MY DAUGHTER IS TAKING OVER!

AND I HAVE A GIFT FOR YOU. I NEED YOU TO UNDERSTAND WHAT IT MEANS TO ME.

"WHEN I LEFT FIRE LAND, I GAVE MY FATHER THE *BÀ KSÖ*, THE BIG BOW. IT IS THE HIGHEST FORM OF RESPECT.

"BUT MY FATHER DID NOT RETURN THE BOW. HE DID NOT GIVE ME HIS BLESSING."

HE SAID IF WE LEFT FIRE LAND, WE WOULD LOSE WHO WE ARE.

THEY NEVER GOT TO SEE ALL OF THIS.

THEY DIDN'T GET TO SEE THAT I *NEVER* FORGOT WE ARE *FIRE*. THIS IS A BURDEN I STILL CARRY.

EMBER, IT IS IMPORTANT THAT YOU KNOW YOU HAVE *MY* BLESSING.

SO I HAD THIS MADE FOR YOU.

WOW, ÀSHFÁ.

EMBER'S FIREPLACE

BUT AS HER FATHER LEAVES, EXCITED FOR THE BIG UNVEILING, HE DOESN'T SEE...

COME, BERNIE, YOU NEED YOUR REST.

EMBER'S

...HIS DAUGHTER *CRY*, A CRACK IN HER FIERY EXTERIOR...

BUT THERE ARE OTHER CRACKS AS WELL.

CRICK

EMBER'S FIREPLACE

THE NEXT DAY...

EMBER! SO WHAT'D YOUR MOM SAY? ABOUT OUR READING?

NOTHING. LOOK, I HAVE A GIFT FOR YOU.

WAIT. WHY ARE YOU GIVING ME GIFTS?

OH NO. NO NO NO NO NO.

HOLD ON. I THINK I HAVE SOMETHING TO SHOW YOU.

A LITTLE WHILE LATER...

WADE, WHAT ARE WE DOING HERE? AND WHY DID I NEED TO WEAR *BOOTS*?

INSIDE THE STATION...

HEY, GALE.

WADE, WHAT'S GOING ON?

I KNOW YOU THINK YOU HAVE TO END THIS, BUT...

DO YOU STILL WANT TO SEE A VIVISTERIA?

GALE BLOWS AN ENORMOUS BUBBLE...

WAIT, I'M SUPPOSED TO GET IN THERE?

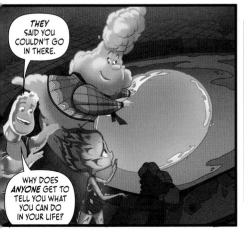

THEY SAID YOU COULDN'T GO IN THERE.

WHY DOES *ANYONE* GET TO TELL YOU WHAT YOU CAN DO IN YOUR LIFE?

SO EMBER GETS IN THE BUBBLE, WITH ABOUT TWENTY MINUTES OF AIR, AND THE JOURNEY BEGINS...

...AND NOT TOO LONG AFTER...

EXPOSED TO EMBER'S GLOW, THE VIVISTERIA *BLOOMS!*

WHOA.

A VIVISTERIA.

AS EMBER RUNS OUT OF AIR IN THE BUBBLE, SHE AND WADE LEAVE THE VIVISTERIA AND THE STATION...

THAT WAS AMAZING.

IT WAS INSPIRING. *YOU* WERE INSPIRING.

AND SLOWLY, CAUTIOUSLY, THEY TOUCH...

NO. WADE, WE CAN'T TOUCH.

MAYBE WE CAN.

LET'S SEE WHAT HAPPENS, AND IF IT'S A DISASTER, THEN WE'LL KNOW THIS WOULD NEVER WORK.

HISSSSS

...PROVING THAT FIRE AND WATER *CAN* BE TOGETHER.

I'M SO LUCKY.

BUT EMBER KNOWS IT CANNOT BE. SHE MUST GO BACK TO HER LIFE AT THE SHOP, WHERE SHE WILL TAKE OVER THE NEXT DAY.

YOU'VE GOT AN OPPORTUNITY TO DO SOMETHING YOU *WANT* WITH YOUR LIFE!

GETTING TO *DO WHAT YOU WANT* IS A LUXURY, AND *NOT* FOR PEOPLE LIKE ME.

I THOUGHT YOU WERE SO STRONG, BUT... YOU'RE JUST AFRAID.

DON'T YOU *DARE* JUDGE ME! YOU DON'T KNOW WHAT IT'S LIKE TO HAVE PARENTS WHO GAVE UP *EVERYTHING* FOR YOU!

I'M *FIRE*, WADE. IT'S OUR WAY OF *LIFE*. I CANNOT THROW ALL THAT AWAY JUST FOR *YOU*.

I DON'T UNDERSTAND!

AND THAT ALONE IS A REASON THIS COULD NEVER WORK. IT'S OVER, WADE.

EMBER RETURNS TO THE SHOP FOR THE GRAND REOPENING...

YOU ARE THE EMBER OF OUR FAMILY FIRE. I AM SO PROUD TO HAVE YOU TAKE OVER MY LIFE'S WORK. THIS IS A LANTERN I BROUGHT FROM THE OLD COUNTRY. TODAY I PASS IT ON TO YOU.

SUDDENLY...

OH BOY.

WADE? WHAT ARE YOU DOING HERE?

THERE ARE A *MILLION* REASONS WHY THIS CAN'T WORK.

A MILLION NOES. BUT THERE'S ALSO ONE YES.

WE TOUCHED. AND WHEN WE DID... WE CHANGED EACH OTHER'S CHEMISTRY.

ENOUGH! WHAT KIND OF FOOD INSPECTION IS THIS? WHO *ARE* YOU?!

JUST A GUY WHO BURST INTO YOUR DAUGHTER'S LIFE IN A FLOODED OLD BASEMENT.

SO YOU *ARE* THE ONE WHO BURST THE PIPES!

DESPITE ALL THEIR EFFORTS TO SAVE THE SHOP, THE WATER PROVES TOO STRONG...

I'M SORRY TO SAY THIS, BUT THE SHOP IS DONE. THE *FLAME* IS DONE.

NO! THIS IS MY FATHER'S WHOLE LIFE! I'M NOT GOING ANYWHERE!

EMBER AND WADE ARE PUSHED INTO THE HEARTH...AND WADE HAS THE LANTERN WITH THE BLUE FLAME!

EMBER AND WADE ARE TRAPPED IN THE CHIMNEY AFTER DEBRIS HAS BLOCKED THE OPENING.

I HAVE TO OPEN THAT UP!

NO! THE WATER WILL COME IN, AND YOU'LL BE SNUFFED OUT.

BUT YOU'RE *EVAPORATING!*

I DON'T KNOW WHAT TO DO!

IT'S OKAY. I HAVE NO REGRETS. YOU GAVE ME SOMETHING PEOPLE SEARCH FOR THEIR WHOLE LIVES.

BUT I CAN'T EXIST IN A WORLD WITHOUT YOU! I'M SORRY I DIDN'T SAY IT BEFORE.

I LOVE YOU, WADE.

I REALLY DO LOVE IT WHEN YOUR LIGHT DOES THAT.

EVENTUALLY, THE FLOODWATER RECEDES...BUT BERNIE'S SHOP IS DESTROYED.

MONTHS LATER, ALL HAS BEEN RESTORED...AND BERNIE'S SHOP HAS BECOME A GATHERING PLACE FOR EVERYONE!

BERNIE HAS FOUND SOMEONE *ELSE* TO RUN THE SHOP.

AND AS WADE ARRIVES...

EMBER, IT'S TIME.

...IT IS TIME FOR GOODBYES.

DAD, I'M SORRY THE INTERNSHIP IS SO FAR AWAY. BUT IT MIGHT NOT END UP BEING ANYTHING—

SHHH. GO. START A NEW LIFE. YOUR MOTHER AND I WILL BE HERE.

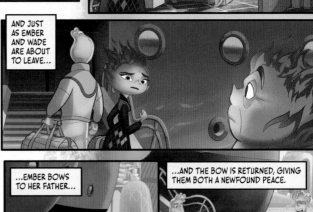

AND JUST AS EMBER AND WADE ARE ABOUT TO LEAVE...

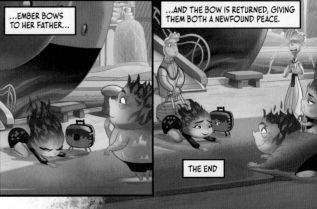

...EMBER BOWS TO HER FATHER...

...AND THE BOW IS RETURNED, GIVING THEM BOTH A NEWFOUND PEACE.

THE END

There's a word in **Firish**: *Tìshók*. It means "**Embrace the light while it burns, 'cause it won't always last forever.**"

—Ember

Just take a
breath
and make a
connection.

—Bernie

GRAPHIC NOVEL

SCRIPT ADAPTATION
Steve Behling

LAYOUT
Emilio Urbano

INK
Marco Forcelloni,
Manuela Razzi, Gianfranco Florio

COLOR
Massimo Rocca, Silvano Scolari,
Maaw Illustration

LETTERS
Chris Dickey

COVER

LAYOUT
Emilio Urbano

INK
Marco Forcelloni

COLOR
Massimo Rocca

DISNEY PUBLISHING WORLDWIDE
Global Magazines, Comics, and Partworks

PUBLISHER
Lynn Waggoner

EXECUTIVE EDITOR
Carlotta Quattrocolo

EDITORIAL TEAM
Bianca Coletti (Director, Magazines),
Guido Frazzini (Director, Comics),
Stefano Ambrosio (Executive Editor),
Camilla Vedove (Senior Manager,
Editorial Development),
Behnoosh Khalili (Senior Editor),
Julie Dorris (Senior Editor),
Kendall Tamer (Assistant Editor),
Cristina Casas (Assistant Editor)

DESIGN
Enrico Soave (Senior Designer)

ART
Roberto Santillo (Creative Director),
Marco Ghiglione (Creative Manager),
Stefano Attardi (Illustration Manager)

PORTFOLIO MANAGEMENT
Olivia Ciancarelli (Director)

BUSINESS & MARKETING
Mariantonietta Galla
(Senior Manager, Franchise),
Virpi Korhonen (Editorial Manager)

GRAPHIC DESIGN
Chris Dickey

EDITORIAL WRITING
Steve Behling

CONTRIBUTOR
Simona Grandi

SPECIAL THANKS
Scott Tilley, Nick Balian